THE BLESSING,
OF ANIMALS

THE BLESSING
OF ANIMALS

Poems, prayers, reflections and stories

Neil Paynter (ed)

wild goose
publications

www.**ionabooks**.com

Contents of book © individual contributors
Compilation © Neil Paynter

First published 2025 by
Wild Goose Publications
Suite 9, Fairfield
1048 Govan Road, Glasgow G51 4XS, Scotland
A division of Iona Community Trading CIC
Limited Company Reg. No. SC156678
www.ionabooks.com

ISBN 978-1-80432-400-4

Cover photo © Artbitz | Dreamstime.com

Printed in the UK by Page Bros (Norwich) Ltd

MIX
Paper | Supporting
responsible forestry
FSC® C023114

Contents

Poems

Prayers

Reflections and stories

For Stevie

POEMS

Christmas 2020

'… resting against the naked breast of life …'
~ Etty Hillesum

As I do, the little birds
tough out winter here
in frozen hills enfolding
the Ohio River valley,
today puff up like oranges
that were always tucked
way down in the tippy toes
of our Christmas stockings.

This frigid, festal morning
on two sides of the feeder
a bright, crimson cardinal,
an ordinary brown sparrow
pick toward the corner.
They will meet, nibbling
their unearned, freely given
Christmas breakfast.

Both are cold and hungry, but
neither drives the other away
from wizened, stippled seeds
that once were summer's
glorious, golden sunflowers,
now being transformed
into a feathered fluttering
that presses bravely toward life

as, in another dark winter,
did a refugee boy in Bethlehem
against the gratuitous gift
of his mother's warm breast.

Bonnie Thurston

Feathered friends

In spite of the heat
it has been a summer
of ten species before breakfast,
increasing avian activity
especially the week after
the hill was mowed.

Birdsong is vesper hymn,
for a solitude so fulsome
it is not harmed but enhanced
by the whisper of wings,
by the broken blue egg
beneath the lilac.

Bonnie Thurston

Winter's breakfast guests

After the first heavy snow
I provide birdseed in the lilac
outside my study window
for the charming distraction
when five or six species
flutter around the feeder,
decorate barren branches.
The littlest birds are bravest,
perch on the window sill,
look inquisitively at me, or
admire themselves in the glass.

This morning, all but one bird
suddenly arose and took flight
up into the snowy woods.
A hawk (or harrier?) landed
in a sycamore across the field
to watch for a breakfast
of his smaller cousins.
No wonder the solitary nuthatch
clung motionlessly to its branch.
Sometimes it is wisest
to do nothing at all.

Bonnie Thurston

Words like birds

Like ordinary garden variety
birds around the house,
and, like them, often
in the early morning,
words sometimes sing to me.
Not obscure, Latinate ones,
but plainer ones, the robins,
and sparrows of language,
words about the senses,
and what they teach,
words about the importance
of daily, domestic life:
the well-made nest,
a luscious worm,
gratuitous crumbs,
the launching of fledglings
from the nest's safety
into a dangerous world.
Like the warbling wren
who lives in the eaves,
who, as I do, rises early,
some simple words carry
a symphony of meaning
in a tiny puff of sound.

Bonnie Thurston

Sutton's warbler, unconfirmed sighting

Unlike pudgy chickadees
with whom it shared the feeder,
this bird had a peculiar beauty,
an elegant, sleek body,
daffodil-yellow throat,
grey coat over snowy shirt,
kohl under, white shadow
above its tiny, avian eyes.
It even ate delicately,
singularly, without mate
or observable companion.
Yes, I know. It is a rarity.
Peterson says 'not expected'.
This may be the wrong place,
and I am no ornithologist.
Officialdom didn't recognise
the Son of God either.
But the *laoi* knew
what they had seen.

Bonnie Thurston

Rats

Why did God create rats?
Destructive, dirty, vicious, red-eyed, flea-ridden,
disease-carrying pests.
Wouldn't the world be better off without them?
But ...
How many drugs and medications
have been tested on laboratory rats?
How many advances in the understanding
of animal physiology and behaviour
came from experiments on rats?
In Cambodia, giant rats (the stuff of nightmares?)
are helping to clear landmines from fields.
Those who have kept pet rats
(such people do exist, I am one of them),
say that their pets are clean, intelligent,
affectionate companions.
And they don't have red eyes ...
Or fleas.

Brian Ford

Dancing in the desert

Wild animals attended him. (Remembered Bible)

I like to imagine Jesus
dancing in the desert,
forty days and nights
of strictly gone wild:

a samba with a mamba,
a foxtrot with a fox,
eyeing up an ibex,
gazing at a gazelle,
sticking to a gecko,
hopping with a sandhopper,
digging a hole with a golden mole.
That's a perfect score from me!

Janet Lees

Everybody knows that cats like to rumba

Eels like to shimmy
and cows do a hoedown
rhinos hornpipe and
hippos can hula
but everybody knows that cats like to rumba

Pollywogs can cakewalk
flamingos can cancan
dingos tango
peacocks fandango
mongooseys watusi
and wapitis dance boppity

but everybody knows that cats like to rumba
everybody knows that cats like to rumba

Mambas mambo
molluscs mazurka
llamas samba and
pandas La Bamba
Wonga-wongas like to conga conga
but everybody knows that cats like to rumba

Foxes like a trot
German shepherds polka
bunnies bunny hop
bugs like to jitter
ducks disco
swordfish sword dance
tapirs caper and civets
and vervets curvet
but everybody knows that cats like to rumba

Chimps do the monkey
worms do the worm
wombats do the wild wildebeest
shaggy horses clog dance
polar bears like a snowball
hairy black spiders tarantella
but everybody knows that cats like to rumba

Emus and gnus boogaloo
rattlesnakes shake their booties
bees do the honey dance
bears are chained to waltzes
svelte silky impalas saraband
colourful coral fish calypso
but everybody knows that cats like to rumba

Giraffes gavotte and
guinea pigs dance the Irish gig
lambs do the fling in spring
whales ballet
newborn things do the hokey-cokey
but everybody knows that cats like to rumba
everybody knows that cats like to rumba

Camels do the bump bump bump
skunks are full of funk funk funk
amoebas pair off
boas hold their last dance close
stinkbugs cut a mean rug
porcupines dance alone mostly
whelks and elks got nothing in common much
but everybody knows that cats like to rumba

Lemmings mosh and
drakes do a slam dance
beetles twist and shout and shake it up baby now
but everybody knows that cats like to rumba

Gypsy moths dance by caravan light
Shetland ponies like a ceilidh
baboons ballroom and
ants like a march tune
centipedes have to be careful and
millipedes have to be carefuller
but everybody knows that cats like to rumba
everybody knows that cats like to rumba
everybody knows that cats like to rumba!

Neil Paynter

Blackstone's journey

Loud, persistent protests
as we set off from St Ives
on the long journey to the Western Isles;
the vociferous indignation
turning into intermittent pleas,
plaintive, compelling.
Out of his basket at every stop,
his elongated body sees all
through the windows.
Is he memorising his route home?
Every return to his basket
an unequal struggle.
Occasionally a paw stretches out,
scratches my arm – a reminder.
An overnight stop – no respite or rest
for driver or passenger.
The last lap – the ferry;
the movements and vagaries of the sea.
Snoring gently,
curled neatly into a ball,
a paw holding down an unruly tail;
comfortable on an uneven lap.
A picture of contentment,
settling into his new home.

Katherine Rennie

Blackstone's love

Lying in bed,
feverish and out of sorts,
a sudden weight on my feet:
Blackstone has joined me.
Purring softly he curls up,
his body warm against mine;
here to share my misery,
to keep me company,
to watch over me.
His way of showing love.

Katherine Rennie

Emptiness

The soft dark body no longer
dominates my bed.
Silence permeates every
corner of my home.
No intermittent thuds,
well-balanced crash-landings
from different launch pads.
No persistent complaints
at delayed meals or unsatisfactory food.
No pained looks from a cosy curled-up ball
at my late homecomings.
I miss him terribly.

Katherine Rennie

Eyes

The eyes have it! The eyes have it!

I'm good with my eyes.
I can do, 'You're my favourite person in the whole world,
you are,' with my eyes.
And it usually works.

The eyes have it! The eyes have it!

I can do, 'I am so disappointed in your lack of attention,'
with my eyes,
when it doesn't work –
and usually that works too.
The eyes have it! The eyes have it!

I can do, 'I'm sorry I messed up.
I promise I won't do it again,' with my eyes,
when I'm about to be sent to bed.
That usually calms things down.
The eyes have it! The eyes have it!

I can do, 'I'm delighted with you today,' with my eyes,
and a wagging tail helps too.
Oh, the smile and the tummy-rub I get for that!
The eyes have it! The eyes have it!

I can tell when she's happy. She can do that with her eyes,
and a grin, and a 'Good boy!'
Happy with me, or just happy?
The eyes have it! The eyes have it!

I can tell when she's down. She can do that with her eyes,
and her tears, and her pleading look,

the one that tells me she needs me to cuddle in.
The eyes have it! The eyes have it!

I can tell when she's not in the mood for me.
She can do that with her eyes,
and the head-shake, and the drooping shoulders,
and the weary eyes, always the eyes.
The eyes have it! The eyes have it!

She says, 'You're the only one who understands me.'
She can do that with her eyes.
She speaks, but she doesn't need words.
I just know. I can tell.
The eyes have it! The eyes have it!

Eyes that speak.
Eyes that know.
Eyes that feel.
Eyes that hurt.

Eyes of hope.
Eyes of death.
Eyes of life.
Eyes of fight.

Eyes that show.
Eyes that sing.
Eyes that yearn.
Eyes that moan.

Eyes of fire.
Eyes of light.
Eyes of wonder.
Eyes of grace.
Eyes that smile.

Eyes that glance.
Eyes that stare.
Eyes that see.
Hers and mine.

Aye, the eyes have it!
The eyes have it! Right enough.

Tom Gordon

Patience

I'll just put a paw on his knee … gently … not too pushy …
Nothing.

I'll wait.
Nothing.

I know what'll work … I'll do the pleading eyes bit.
Nothing.

A little whine, perhaps?
'Will you stop that!'

Well, at least that's something. He knows I'm here …
So, I'll wait.
Nothing.

A whine?
'I've told you already … Not now! Go to bed!'

Now?
Nothing.

I'll try the paw again.
Nothing.

I'll wait.
Nothing.

Two paws, and a whine, and the pleading eyes?
'Oh ...'

Oh yes! This could be it! If I throw in the biggest tail-wag ever,
it might ...
'Oh, for goodness' sake. You *are* a pest!
But, up you come, if you must ... here ... beside me on the sofa.
Now, will that do? Settle down, right?'

Yes!
Success!
It's amazing what you can achieve
when you have patience ...

Tom Gordon

Feline theology

I sit at my desk clutching my mug of tea,
staring grimly at incomprehensible jargon on my PC,
trying to make sense of the Hebrew and Greek on the screen.
Do I really understand what the word 'anathema' might mean?
A thesis on the imprecatory psalms, 12,000 words to be written.
At first it seemed a stimulating intellectual challenge,
    now I'm less smitten.
What the difference between vindictive and vindication?
Or election and predestination?

I tug at the remains of my thinning, unbarbered hair.
Do I know? Do I care?
An interruption – the cat butts my leg with her head;
an intercession, she's asking for her daily bread.
I know that it's Whiskas she wants but the principle is the same.
She emits a low-pitched, growling sound, is she calling my name?
Does she regard me as a benevolent deity or merely a gravy train?
Even if she could I doubt if she'd bother to explain.
It's not just food she's after, she wants to sit on my knee –
showing love and affection and expecting the same from me?
Here's a dissertation thesis question to discuss and refine.
Is her theology in any way different from mine?

Brian Ford

Theology lessons

Theology lesson number one:
'What is unconditional love?'

What's your dog like,
when you're in a rotten mood,
or you've screwed up,
or your self-esteem is on the floor,
and your dog
wheedles its nose under your arm,
with a tail going at a million wags to the minute,
and you see in his eyes that you,
even you,
are the most important person in the entire world?
That's unconditional love, OK?

Theology lesson number two:
'What is forgiveness?'

What are you like,
when the puppy has chewed your new slipper,
and you shout, 'No!'
and for a nanosecond
the pooch thinks you're awful,
and then you say,
'Come here you!'
and the bundle of fluff licks your hand,
and your neck, and your face,
and you know this is the best dog in the whole world?
That's forgiveness, right?

Theology lesson number three:
'What is salvation?'

What's it like
when you've fallen into a depression,
and you don't want to face another day,
but there's a dog to walk,
and a dog to feed,
and a dog to love you
even when you don't want to be loved,
and you rouse yourself to do what needs to be done,
before you withdraw again for a time,
till your dog needs to be your saviour again?
That's salvation, here and now.

Theology lesson number four:
'What are blessings?'

A dog who watches where the ball's been thrown,
and actually brings it back.

A dog-walker who doesn't know your name
but knows your dog's name,
and speaks to you when no one else does.
A dog snoring peacefully on the rug by the fire,
exuding contentment
without doing anything else,
communicating that all is well with the world,
and with you.
That's your blessings, all the time.

Tom Gordon

Unconditional

My spell-checker
doesn't correct words
that are spelled correctly but
might be the wrong word.
I once wrote in a prayer,
'My dog loves me unconditionally.'
It should have been God, of course, but
my spell-checker didn't know that.
I was happy with that though.
My dog loving me unconditionally
was as close to God's love
as I needed to be today.
So it looks like my spell-checker
knows more about love
than I give it credit for.
But then, maybe it's my dog
who deserves the credit.

Tom Gordon

Gibbs is my spiritual director

curled up in a
tight little ball
in the sunlight
of a winter day,
you challenge me
to take a needed nap

climbing up in my
lap as i tap away
furiously on my keyboard,
you purr that there
is more to life than work

racing up and down
the hallway chasing some
shadow that only you can
see, you call me to enjoy
the simple things of the day

sitting next to me
with your paw resting
comfortably on my leg
as i slowly turn the page
of a book which has nothing
to do with my calling, you
are content that i am slowly
starting to catch on as to
how to live.

Thom M. Shuman

Sniffing

What is it about my dog sniffing
a random patch of grass?
No food there?
No stick to fetch?
No poo to smell?
Nothing!
Just grass,
the same grass that covers the whole of the park
from end to end and side to side;
the same grass that my dog has explored
in minute detail
every time she's visited her playground.
What does she know is there
that I can't see,
that makes her so fascinated,
so engrossed,
so tied to a few blades of grass
that are more important than millions of others?
'Come on, you!' I cry.
'Keep going!' I cajole.
'Here, girl!' I instruct – moving on.
But she's not ready yet,
not when there are other delights to explore,
much more yet to discover …
After all, isn't the world just wonderful
when you're a dog,
fascinated by random patch of grass –
you can see beyond seeing.

Tom Gordon

Robins

There is a collective noun for flocks of robins,
but it is hardly ever used, or needed.
Ornithologists tell us that a robin in winter
is a solitary bird,
ferociously defending its territory,
viciously attacking other robins.
But in my back garden,
on Boxing Day,
a small rouge (yes that is a collective noun) of robins
fed peacefully together
on the dried mealworms I had provided.
Did they have enough sense not to waste time fighting
when there was enough food for all?
Perhaps God's creation is more peaceful
and harmonious than we think.
Perhaps we just haven't noticed that.

Brian Ford

I dream of Ginger

(To those who dream about their pets)

I dream of Ginger, my childhood dog,
over thirty years since she's been gone.
We're playing, embracing, cuddling on the floor,
though I'll skip over the part where she's talking.

We got her at the start of my kindergarten year,
and she died while I was in college.

Having never gone to school without her,
I grew up as a child of my dog.

Unaware, as I was, of my own father's grief,
who drove her by himself to her sleep,
I received a note from my parents soon after,
affirming that my childhood was gone.

Can memories convey the life of my dog,
or capture the feelings that linger?
The good and the bad – and the bad becomes funny –
as now every memory is treasured.

Leaving a hoodie in the yard, she would chew it.
She'd snatch chicken from our hands in the car.
Following my dad as he tilled the spring garden,
eating grub worms as they surfaced in the dirt.

I wrote stories about her in high school;
I sang songs about her at camp.
And she rose to fame – at least in my head –
as 'Ginger the Amazing Dog'.

Now twenty and thirty years and forty year later,
grief isn't grief as it was.
Still my sense of loss still isn't settled,
and my memories aren't finished letting go.

So, I dream of Ginger, my childhood dog,
rendezvous arranged in the night.
We play, embrace and cuddle on the floor.
Then I listen to what Ginger has to say.

Rodney Aist

Dusty's eyes

The mournful look
at 3:00 in the morning
as if to say, 'sorry to be
such a bother, but i
need to go outside'

the head on the lap
with those deep-brown
eyes gazing so intently
wondering if i might
be able to spare just
a few moments for a cuddle

the delight which sparkles
as you open your eyes
wide to try to see that
squirrel before it sees you
or spot the little kid
coming down the street
who offers the best ear scratches

the gaze you offer in trust
as i look into that soul
as old as creation as i
cradle you in tearful love
while you take your last breath
before journeying back to
stardust.

Thom M. Shuman

Mourning

I cried when the cat died.
It wasn't my cat.
I'm not really a 'cat person'.
And I had no great affection for the little thing.
Kola was my daughter's cat,
the one she couldn't take to college;
the one we had to look after;
the one that was no bother really;
the one that got sick;
the one the vet said should be 'put to sleep'.

So, we took Kola to the vet for the last time.
I say we,
but it was my wife really.
She's a 'cat person' more than me,
a surrogate mother in my daughter's absence.
But I was there too.
'For support,' I said.
'Being around,' I said.
Doing the being-helpful thing,
the 'not-a-cat-person' thing.

The vet was lovely.
The end was peaceful for Kola.
My wife was fine.
And I wept on the way home.
I cried when the cat died,
though I wasn't a cat person.
I cried when the cat died,
and I'm more of a cat person now.

Tom Gordon

Preferences

'Are you a cat person or a dog person?' she asked.
'What?' I replied.
'A cat person or a dog person?' she demanded.
'Neither,' I replied.
'You don't like cats or dogs, or you don't mind either way?'
she continued.
'Neither,' I replied.
'What?' she asked.
'Neither. I like dogs rather than cats, if you must know,' I replied.
'So, you're a dog person,' she asserted.
'No,' I replied.
'What?' she asked.
'I'm not a dog person,' I replied.
'But you said you prefer dogs,' she affirmed.
'I do,' I replied.
'So, you're a dog person then,' she continued.
'No! I'm a person who likes dogs,' I replied.
'So, a dog person,' she insisted.
'No. I'm a people person.
I'm a person, and this person happens to like dogs
rather than cats,' I replied.
'Oh! I see what you mean,' she said.
'I think we'd better start this conversation again,' I replied.
'Are you a hamster person or a gerbil person?' she asked.
'I'm losing the will to live,' I replied.

Tom Gordon

Even the sparrow

'Even the sparrow has found a home, and the swallow a nest for herself … a place near your altar, Lord Almighty.' (Psalm 84:3–4)

Sparrows are allowed in God's house,
welcomed,
with their ceaseless, rowdy noise,
monotonous, inane chirruping
and constant chattering quarrels.
And swallows,
their mud nests spoiling the simple beauty of the walls,
and piles of their smelly, messy, unhygienic droppings
dirtying the floor.

Maybe there are geckos,
climbing the walls,
clinging upside down to ceilings,
so that they see everything
the wrong way up.

Suppose we cleared them all out,
replaced them with rows of well-dressed, respectable people,
smart, fashionable, but not gaudy?
Mannequins.
A shop window for our religion?
Or a beautiful, silent, peaceful
mausoleum?

Brian Ford

Extinct

As dead as a dodo,
as passé as a passenger pigeon,
as gone as a great auk,
as departed as the dinosaurs,
as expired as an ex-parrot:
we only get one chance
to tread gently on the earth
in the company of all creation.

Janet Lees

I know a cat (A skipping poem)

I know a cat whose name is Mimi
she doesn't like tuna fish
I know a cat whose name is Mimi
what's her favourite dish?

(skip:)

Pears
Potatoes
Pizza pie
Falafels
Capers
Ham on rye

Olives
Pickles
Fried bananas
Rumballs

Gumballs
Dried sultanas

I know a cat whose name is Mingy
who likes his mozzarella stringy

I know a cat whose name is Leroy
who left the duck and ate
the decoy

I know a cat named Siamese Sam
who's lost his yen for corned beef and Spam
I know a cat named Siamese Sam
what sticks to his chops?

(skip:)

Blue cheese
Toasted fleas
Chocolate-covered honeybees

Garter snakes
Frosted flakes
Pistachio-almond honeycakes

I know a cat named Need-a-tail
who's trying to eat a lot of kale

I know a cat whose name is Oopik
who forgets how to hunt walrus and seal
I know a cool cat named Oopik Toopik
what's his favourite meal?

Cheese nachos
All-dressed tacos

Enchiladas
Fried iguanas
Beef burritos
Fried Tostitos
Corn tortillas
Margaritas
Hot peppers! *(skip like mad)*

I know a cat whose name is Kate
who plays with the sunlight on her plate

I know a cat whose name's Mad Manx
who struts from his bowl and never says thanx

I know a cat titled Rex the Third
who says that eating canned food's absurd
I know a cat titled Rex the Third
what does he rather fancy?

(skip:)

Pheasant
Quail
Chinchilla under glass

Bouillabaisse
Mayonnaise
Refined sugar

I know a Tom who's a tough Maine Coon
who picks at the garbage and cries at the moon

I know a cat named Davy Crockett
who keeps liquorice jerky in his pocket

I know a cat who's an opera singer
and always wears black coat and tail
I know a cat, half-alto, part-tenor,
what does he like for dinner?

Rigatoni
Rice-A-Roni
Fried baloney
Cold spumoni
Manicotti
Pavarotti
Late Puccini
Hot linguini
Cannelloni
Macaroni
Vermicelli
Cold spaghetti
Hot peppers! *(skip like mad)*

I know a cat who likes a good pot luck
I know a cat who likes a good pot lick

I know a cat who smelt the smelts
(in the salty, fishy, kitcheny air)

I know a cat who's fond of airline peanuts

I know a cat whose name is Stevie
who crunches on Spice Mice watching late-night TV

I know a cat called Hate-to-Cook
who'd rather shed on her deep, soft bed
I know a cat named Hate-to-Cook
what does she like instead?

(skip:)

Take out
Drive through
Ready to eat

Dine in
Phone-up
Delivery free

I know a cat who likes to lie
and dream of eating pie in the sky

I know a cat called Judy Star
who lives for caviar by soft guitar
I know a feline called Judy Star

I know a cat who's kinda finicky
I know a cat who's kinda picnicy

I know a cat who sucks out the marrow
I know a cat who picks like a sparrow

I know a jaded Abyssinian
who doesn't want to eat the same thing again

I know a cat who hisses at hot dogs

I know a cat who relishes relishes

I know the cat who owns Captain Cat Burgers
(but his name is Ed)

I know a cat who chatters for chocolate
I know a cat who's a milkaholic

I know a cat named Alabamy Sammy
whose vit'ls consist of grits and groats

I know a cat named Hamish McCaindish
who always eats stiff Quaker Oats

I know a cat who skips double Dutch
and never even stops for lunch
I know a cat who skips much double Dutch
and never even stops for lunch
and never even stops for lunch …

Neil Paynter

The last return of the prodigal

I'd be the first to admit
he wasn't much of a pet.
I only took him in because his owners were moving away
and couldn't take him with them.
Once here he decided that he'd had enough of humans.
He'd never come when he was called,
he'd turn up for meals
if he felt like it,
sneer and snarl at me
(I can't ever remember hearing him purr)
or, if he felt inclined,
scratch and bite.
I still have the scars from the time
I tried to put him in a cat box
to take him to the vet.
But when he went missing for three days

I was worried.
I searched the garden and nearby streets,
asked the neighbours if they'd seen him.
Then one evening I found him lying in the drive,
hardly able to move,
obviously dying.
I wrapped him in a blanket and put him in his bed.
Characteristically he staggered out
and hid under a bookcase,
and twenty minutes later
he was dead.
I was grateful that the prodigal
had at least wanted to come home to die.

Brian Ford

Toby

Three times I drove past the door,
and three times I simply couldn't bring myself
to open it and carry her inside.
'But she's tired.
Her heart is finished.
You're not doing her any kindness,'
they kept on telling me,
and of course, I knew that what they were saying
was perfectly true.
But the thought of ending her life
was too much for me to handle:
the idea of her death,
and doing without her,
too difficult to embrace.

The well-worn arguments went round and round and round.
'What right do I have to choose the very moment?'
'She does not possess the power to object or refuse.'
'Where is my authority to make this final, fatal decision?'
'Ignorant and unaware,
if she knew what were being suggested,
would she consent and agree?'
'She's only a dog.'
I could easily have punched him.
'You can get another one,' said someone else.
It made me feel sick to the pit.
They didn't understand.
They had never been there.
They had never experienced the reality.
She was my loving companion,
my most forgiving friend,
the apple of both my eyes.
But it had to be done:
movements more painful;
vomiting more frequent;
hearing absent, and sight all but gone;
a leaky heart;
the obvious restlessness;
and now weak groans of discomfort
from deep inside.
The time had come:
the time for death.
It had to be done.

***

It was quick, it was gentle, it was kind
(or so I kept on telling myself).

As the needle went in,
I held her warm little body tightly.
The muscles relaxed,
and power departed,
and the heart stopped beating.
She sank onto the table and lay there lifeless,
and I tickled her ears,
and I made loving noises
as tears fell on her head.

***

From out of nowhere –
it struck me with all the force of a tidal wave.
I knew I'd be upset,
but never for a single moment did I anticipate
the gutting grief would be as intense and painful
as experienced now.
Uncontrollable sobbing.
A whole night without a wink of sleep.
Heart ripped in two, soul tormented, internalised writhing,
self-reproach and feelings of guilt.
What joy can be left?
Family is understandably concerned.
Wife suggests doctor.
'Don't be stupid!' the terse and dismissive reply.
Friend contacted, and arrives post-haste bearing whisky.
(True friends usually know exactly what to do!)
The next day, summoned daughter makes
well-intentioned suggestions:
'Distraction therapy, a change of scene,
we're going on an outing:
Christmas shopping – so let's get cracking,

and put on your coat.'
But memory of it now is scarily absent;
coffee and bacon rolls in café erased from thought and mind.

***

So this is the grief I've heard them talking about.
And this is the nature of loss and unbearable pain
which others have known.
This the twilight zone when absence of happiness
is a torturing reality.
And this is the black-dog day
when no one has a right to say:
'She was only a dog.'

***

Can there be healing?
Will time make it better?
Can there ever be total mending and perfect repair?
For still I pine for her.
Still I ache to feel her sitting on my lap.
Still I wish I could touch those soft, brown ears
and look into those faithful brown eyes,
and witness the stump of a tail wagging vigorously
in unconditional acceptance.
It's true that passing time
has removed something of the sting and much of the sharpness.
But not for a minute can I ever believe
that the healing will be total and complete.

Glendon Macaulay

PRAYERS

The God of all creatures

Yes! We will praise God!
We will praise God in dog-parks.
We will praise God in paddocks.
Yes! We will praise God!

We will praise God in our aquariums.
We will praise God from our perches.
A little boy with a purring cat on his lap,
a young girl teaching a puppy to roll over,
an old woman conversing with her pretty parrot,
an old man cleaning out the rabbit hutch –
let them all praise God's name!

Yes! We praise the God of all creatures!

Thom M. Shuman

Bless to me my dog

God of all living creatures,
bless to me my dog:
a constant friend,
whose 'I love you'
is wordless,
who gives and greets
guides and protects
unconditionally.

Joy Mead

Bless my cat

Bless my cat
for she is the pinnacle of creation:

Bless her wildness and warmth,
bless her long fur,
bless her tail of great worth,
bless her ability to snore,
bless her considered dedication to Felix,
bless her company,
bless her thunderous purr,
bless her finding of me,
bless her utter catness,
bless her sharpened claw.

Bless, God of felines,
all who travel their way,
night and day,
through the open cat door.

Rosie Miles

The blessings of birds

When the birds sing you to your rest,
when the crows fly to their nests
and starlings murmur their magic over the sky,
you know you are blessed.
May God grant a quiet night
and a perfect end.

Janet Lees

Awareness

What is it with dogs,
crashed out on the fireside rug
after a long walk,
and hearing a car-door slam
two streets away,
and immediately up and listening,
in case this might be something new for them?

Awareness.

What is it with dogs,
sleeping the sleep of the just,
yet up and interested,
ready for action,
at my slightest twitch,
while I struggle to get up
from my comfy chair and get motivated?

Awareness.

What is it with dogs
who can't speak, but know;
who can't ask questions, but understand;
who can't cry, but look sad;
who can't say 'Sorry!', but know when they're forgiven;
who demand little, but give a lot;
who can read me, even when I can't read myself?

Awareness.

Today I pray for awareness –
just a little bit of awareness –
like that.

Amen

Tom Gordon

Why are you doing this?

Barking like a maniac
sniffing at every tree and blade of grass
chasing everything that moves
sleeping and snoring the rest of the time …
Why are you doing this?

Meowing pathetically
purring affectionately
running crazily
sleeping endlessly …
Why are you doing this?

Beloved companion,
who greets me when I go and when I come.
Who sits with me when I eat and when I read.
Who sleeps with me wherever I am.
Who irritates me and comforts me,
keep doing this.

O beloved companion,
I do not know why you do this

but I pray you will never stop.
You calm me when I am lonely.
You heal my heart when it is broken.
You give me peace when I cannot rest.
Keep doing this, I pray.

Rebeka Maples

Thank you

Thank you, God,
for a dog that can fetch and bring,
and ask for no reward,
other than to be asked
to fetch and bring some more –
teaching me about giving for the sake of giving.

Thank you, God,
for a dog that forgives me
when I'm grumpy,
and allows me to love again
even when I don't feel like loving –
teaching me that I can be restored to what I should be.

Thank you, God,
for a dog that thinks it's God
when I feed her,
so that she is fully what she should be
because I care –
teaching me about how to make people feel they matter.

Thank you, God,
for a dog that shows me what
stillness is like,
knowing that activity is over for now,
even for a moment –
teaching me about rest and letting go.

Thank you, God,
for a dog that allows me to believe
that today is a new day,
full of possibilities,
and yesterday is over and gone –
teaching me about hope, and life, and wonder.
Amen

Tom Gordon

Bless us, O Lord

Bless us, O Lord,
our wagging and our drooling,
our jumping and our scratching,
our eating and our sleeping.
When we sit, help us to wait patiently,
not to whine or beg,
and forgive us when we don't get it right.

When the thunder roars,
let us know that you are near.
When the door opens
and our forever friend returns,

let us know that food and love are here,
in the day and in the night.

Bless us, O Lord;
guide us inside and outside,
on our lead and off,
as we follow you into the light.
Amen

Rebeka Maples

A stag beetle on the Greenwich Meridian Trail

Having walked over ninety miles
along a random line,
I am thankful, on the final lap,
to meet one of the largest insects in Britain.
Its lacquered beauty, shiny armour,
feathered antennae and scuttling gait
are a joy to encounter on the sloping path.
God bless the diversity of our planet.
May we get the balance right for all species.

Janet Lees

Keep moving

May you beetle along bravely.
May you lollop along lovingly.
May you pounce positively
and bounce beautifully.

Leap like a lynx,
spring like a gazelle,
swoop like an owl,
dive like a gannet,
bound, jump and twirl
in the company of all our kindred.

Janet Lees

For ordinary wonderful things

Thank you, God, for the kiss of a dog's wet nose and
for the purring contentedness of a cat.
For these ordinary wonderful things –
thank you, God.

May we never forget to give thanks to you,
Maker and Giver of all.
Amen

Richard Sharples

REFLECTIONS
AND STORIES

St Hubert and the stag

Stags and deer abound in the imagery of the Bible and in the folklore of many lands. In medieval times they were associated with a number of saints and with Christ himself. There are several stories of conversion experiences through encounter with this mysterious creature, one of which concerns St Hubert.

Hubert was the eldest son of the Duke of Aquitaine in the south-west of medieval France. He revelled in the vivacity of court life until the day his wife died in childbirth, whereupon, grief-stricken, he plunged himself into hunting, which soon became an obsession. One Good Friday, when most were at church, Hubert set out to the forest with his hounds. Giving chase to a great stag, he eventually cornered it in a thicket, but rather than struggling to escape, the stag solemnly faced his hunter, telling him he was doomed unless he turned to God and embraced a holy life. Shining between his antlers was a crucifix. Shamed into repentance, Hubert did indeed commit himself to the church and became renowned as a man of peace.

Hubert's Damascus moment, his transforming experience, came about through the animal kingdom. He experienced Christ in the hunted victim. The mindless killing in which he had lost himself was a wound to Christ who is all and in all. Each creature's life is precious to God; not a sparrow falls without God knowing, and every wild and domestic creature belongs to God (Matthew 10:29, Psalm 104, Psalm 50, Leviticus 17).

Just imagine the wake-up shock if, like Hubert, we heard Christ speaking through the victims our species is destroying, or has already destroyed. Would it be enough to change any of us? Or what if we were met with a vision of the cross over a supermarket checkout? What if we were suddenly brought to our knees by the realisation of Christ's identification with the suffering of sweatshop workers, the lives destroyed by the felling of rainforests, the factory-farmed animals, the countless victims of a Mammon-worshipping world?

Always Jesus calls us out of violence, as he called Saul, one of his greatest emissaries: 'Saul, Saul, why do you persecute me?' Saul turned all the passion and energy he had once poured into hunting down the followers of Jesus into dynamic, ceaseless love for them, a desire to make known Christ's love, because he was touched by that love himself.

The Christ-stag does not appear simply to make us feel guilty. There is love in his gaze; he wants to save us from ourselves. We are his beloved, remember; he longs for us to come away with him, rejoicing that the spring has come. In contemplating this divine love we might wake up to the longing in our own souls. Like thirsty deer seeking living water, we follow not because we are afraid or because we are ashamed but because there is nowhere we would rather be.

As a deer longs for flowing streams,
so my soul longs for you, O God;
my soul thirsts for you
in a dry and barren land
stripped of vegetation and starved of life,
a land ploughed and pillaged in violence –
how long, O Lord, how long
must this dry waterbed of death
scar the earth
where healing waters ought to flow?
How long, O Lord, how long,
until your little ones see
your kingdom come
on earth, as it is in heaven?
Amen

Annie Heppenstall

An incarnate God

Icy winds were blowing around Scan's abattoir in Linköping on that February morning. I was there with five other Christians concerned about animal welfare, to pray for animals in the livestock industry. We had placed an icon of Christ and some pictures of suffering animals and people against the wall with a couple of candles in front of them. We sat silently on camping mats. From time to time an animal transporter passed a few metres behind us. Suddenly it became completely obvious to me: of course God feels the animals' suffering deep within God's own being! Of course every individual matters to God. How can we humans fail to understand that?

The following day I read in the newspaper that a cow had escaped from Linköping's slaughterhouse earlier that morning. She had just been unloaded from the truck when she jumped over the fence and ran off. For one and a half hours she ran through the industrial area and local housing estates. After a while she had four police vehicles chasing her. On the way down to Lake Roxen she was caught. And killed.

Annika Spalde

Ask the animals

But ask the animals, and they will teach you; the birds of the air, and they will tell you; ask the plants of the earth, and they will teach you; and the fish of the sea will declare to you. Who among all these does not know that the hand of the Lord has done this?'

Job 12:7–9, NRSV

These verses cause me to contemplate further on the extinction of the species. Oh, for the wisdom of Job! What are the animals, the birds, the plants and the fish teaching us today? The list of threatened and endangered species kept by the International Union for the Conservation of Nature (IUCN) is now at over forty thousand, and the list of species that have become extinct increases each year. We all know about the dodo of Mauritius, the American passenger pigeon and the huge ratite birds of New Zealand, but many other lesser-known creatures have also become extinct. Miners used to carry canaries into the mines with them to warn them if a poisonous gas was around and the environment was deadly. Some of the greatest extinctions today are amongst frogs and other amphibians, which are particularly sensitive to environmental change: the death of these species is our warning sign today – but we do not seem to be heeding this.

In the 1970s I had the privilege of visiting a student of mine working in the Monteverde Cloud Forest Preserve in Costa Rica. Since she was studying the pollination of a plant by rice rats we were out in the forest at night. It was the mating time of the beautiful golden toad and I was privileged to see them out scrambling among the roots of the trees. But that is not possible any more as this is one of the amphibian species that has become extinct from drier weather with a distinct dry season. This period of drought never used to occur and is due to the amount of rainforest deforestation in the lowlands of Costa Rica.

What we do in one place affects other places because the environment has no frontiers and depends on the services provided by rainfall, vegetation and many other factors.

Particularly threatened are organisms that are adapted to life on mountains. As a boy I studied the alpine plants of Ben Lawers in Scotland. Today data from the Royal Botanic Garden, Edinburgh shows that, due to climate change, these plants are migrating gradually upwards. Since the mountains are low, there will soon be no climate suitable for these alpines.

In North America the attractive rabbit relative the pika lives on mountaintop boulder fields. Its thick fur-coat keeps it warm in winter, but it dies quickly when temperatures reach around 80 degrees Fahrenheit (26.6°C). As climate change causes temperature to rise, pikas are confined to their 'sky islands' and can't escape. Already pikas have disappeared from some of their mountain habitats.[1] It seems that it is the plants and animals that are well-adapted to the cold which are the first to suffer from what we are doing to the climate, such as the polar bear.

How the world has depleted fish populations because of greedy over-fishing and the pollution of rivers and streams is well known.

We should be listening to the strong message that we are receiving from the animals, birds, plants and fish. We need these creatures as part of our survival strategy, and have no right to destroy what God has given us to use, but not abuse.

Ghillean Prance, former Scientific Director of the Eden Project

Note:
1. Information about pikas from New Scientist, 5 October 2002

God bless you, Dusty

Dusty the Church Dog never met a bad day. If it was snowing, that meant going down to the nearby school and racing around the fields; it meant making doggy snow angels in the front yard, and catching snowballs no matter how hard they were thrown. If it was raining, it meant splashing through puddles, and rolling in the front yard until he was soaked to the skin. If it was a crisp autumn day, it meant walking down around the lake (or perhaps the campground with the great smells) looking for the Biscuit Lady, who always had treats for him. If it was a clear spring day, there was nothing better than sitting on the lawn, smelling the leaves uncurling, the dandelions poking their heads up out of the earth, the birds building their nests in the trees.

Dusty the Church Dog never met a person he didn't immediately like and turn into his new BF. From the curmudgeonly neighbour who always had a frown on his face and a complaint on his lips to the little kid trying out his bicycle with training wheels, Dusty just had to meet them, had to greet them, had to turn their day into the most tail-wagging-est one they had ever had. He enjoyed meeting other dogs, especially the little guys in the neighbourhood, and managed to give a wide berth to any cats he met. Squirrels always found a tree to run up, rabbits always seemed to bounce further when they saw him, and deer utterly confused him.

Dusty the Church Dog touched lives in ways in which I can only dream of doing. He would turn those big brown eyes towards the face of the woman sitting in the hallway at the nursing home, and her face would beam with delight.

He read books by the dozens to kids on Thursday mornings and taught them how much fun it was to catch a carrot in mid-air and crunch it to pieces. He showed incredible patience in waiting for his turn at the ice cream place (but don't try to jump the line in front of him!), and he gave unconditional love and acceptance to everyone he met, even if simply passing on the street.

Dusty the Church Dog was my confidant, my trusted companion, my faithful sidekick, my window into the grace, the love, the wonder, the power, the joy of God which is always around us. He was the one who got me out of bed to listen to the geese flying south. He was the one who taught me that there is always something to experience, someone to meet, some marvellous delight just waiting around the next corner. He was the one who couldn't wait to experience the next moment which was coming into his life. He was the one who got me through some of the toughest days of ministry, of our struggles with Teddy, our son, of life itself.

Sadly, Dusty the Church Dog finally met something that didn't love him, that wouldn't give in to his silly smile and gentle nature, that wouldn't let him keep going through this life. A tumour on his spleen that was causing internal bleeding meant that those who loved him so much and would miss him beyond any possible words could describe, had to help him cross that Rainbow Bridge into peace, gentleness and everlasting joy. So, about an hour ago, we held him, hugged him, whispered our thanks to him as he closed his eyes one last time this side of life.

And you will never, ever convince me that the wet streets and sidewalks we discovered when we came out of the vet's office were simply from a passing shower.

Thom M. Shuman

Scooby

Ever since Millicent had got herself a dog, she'd become part of the fraternity of local dog-walkers. There was no joining fee or membership card. You just appeared with a dog, met other dog-walkers, and you were in. Dog-walkers were nice people. They stopped and had a chat, even on wet days, as your dog and their dog sniffed around each other. They compared notes with you about how your dog was – how old, what breed, quirky temperaments, feeding regimes, and the like. They even recognised you when you were out walking without your dog and greeted you with a nod or a wave or a cheery 'hello'.

But the thing that surprised Millicent was that none of the dog-walkers seemed to know each other's names. You would meet a new dog-walker – just as Millicent had been some months before – and without saying 'Hello, I'm Millicent', or 'I'm sorry, I don't know your name,' you would immediately launch into dog-related chat, and, of course, enquire as to the name of the animal.

So, Millicent knew other dog-walkers as 'Corrie's dad', 'Jemma's mum' and the like, though she had no earthly idea what the owners' names really were.

Millicent's was a big, amiable, slightly mad pooch – a '57 varieties' type – she'd named Scooby. So, of course, Millicent was known in the dog-walking club as 'Scooby's mum'.

Scooby had been Millicent's salvation during her recent depression. She'd not experienced depression before, so she didn't know what she was supposed to think or feel. She just wanted to curl up and hide, pull the duvet over her head and never see another living soul. But she couldn't. Well, there was Scooby, wasn't there? Not that he demanded much, just feeding a couple of times a day – and, of course, his regular walks.

When the depression set in, it was all Millicent could do to drag herself out of bed and take Scooby out in the morning. He didn't seem to mind and was always ready to go, tail wagging, as soon as Millicent had her coat on and his leash in her hand. It was the same at lunchtime. There he was, waiting patiently at the bottom of the stair, eyes bright, twitching to get out – while Millicent felt like hell. But what did a mad mongrel know about depression? All he was bothered about was that Millicent appeared at all, and that he got fed, and that walks were a regular part of his day, and that he knew who looked after him.

With the help of caring medical people, Millicent has come through her depression. But she'll tell you that she'd never have survived if it wasn't for Scooby. He gets longer walks now and gets off the leash in the park too. He's still as mad as ever, and still thinks that the world is totally, fabulously, excitingly, beautifully wonderful every time Millicent puts her coat on and has his leash in her hand.

Now she's more on top of things, Millicent chooses not to think much about her period of depression. But she does give Scooby a big hug sometimes when she remembers how important he'd been for her during her bad spell. She doesn't really bother if the dog-walkers know her name. Because, first and foremost, she's delighted to be known as Scooby's mum.

Tom Gordon

Cocoa the Wonder Dog I

In July 2003, Cocoa the Wonder Dog came into our lives. This was a big step for us (some in the family would say a crazy step), since, being confirmed cat people, we had not really had a relationship with a dog. And, like decisions in many families, this was not a unanimous one.

But it has proven to be a wise choice. For during those long, difficult months of surgery, chemotherapy and hospital stays, which followed our son's diagnosis of Stage 4 cancer, we always had someone at home waiting for us – filled with unconditional love and never-ending hope. I always thought it was true with cats, but Cocoa reminded us that pets are visible signs of that invisible grace God fills us with in each and every moment of our lives.

And Cocoa got us out of the house, especially on those mornings when bed seemed so safe and warm, and on those evenings when all we wanted to do was to veg out in front of the TV. Cats are perfectly content to take care of their business, in their way and time, but dogs – especially a dog like Cocoa – demand to be walked! And so we did – through puddles; in August heat; shuffling through snow, and trying not to slip on the ice underneath – we walked and walked and walked ... And along the way – on starry nights and cloudy days, in times of uncertainty as well as faithfulness, with tears marring our vision and joy bubbling on our lips – God was at work in our lives with the gentle presence of the Holy Spirit, and the healing grace of Jesus Christ.

We have grown accustomed to the belief that healing comes through medication, medical teams, hospitals, wonder treatments. And it does happen that way. But healing also comes in quiet moments: in the gentle hand on a shoulder, in eating a meal prepared by a neighbour, in the prayers of a community of faith, in the silent moments of the night. All too often, however, we are not alert enough to these moments and ways in which the healing power of God is poured upon us.

God does healing work in many remarkable ways, and often through rather 'unremarkable' people, and sometimes, even through a 'dumb animal' like Cocoa.

Note: We had been looking for a dog on and off for months, when we discovered Cocoa. She was the first dog, in all that searching, who came and approached us, rather than our approaching her first. Not long ago there was a story on the news about a study which showed that some dogs have a special 'sense' by which they are able to 'smell' cancer in a person. We adopted Cocoa about two months before our son was diagnosed with cancer, and probably at the time when it was 'growing' within him. Gives one pause.

God's world

In St Matthew's Gospel Jesus introduces animals in his teachings on no less than twenty-seven occasions. Jesus was obviously very familiar with natural history, and the way in which he referred to animals leaves us in no doubt that he had closely observed their behaviour.

Here is a list of some of the animals that Jesus mentioned; they will remind you of his various parables and warnings: sparrows, locusts, dogs, pigs, wolves, sheep, foxes, doves, vipers, fish, camels, donkeys, hens, chicks, vultures, goats, a colt and, finally, a cockerel.

Today, within our urban life, it is tragic that so many people have no connection with or awareness of the natural world. And if one is not aware of an animal or plant species then there is no interest in conserving it.

I have spent my career working with various botanic gardens and am convinced of their mission within the cities of the world. They are rich green spaces full of plants and often birds and sometimes wild animals. All good gardens also have a children's education programme. This is one of the main purposes of the Eden Project in Cornwall.

I well remember taking a group of youngsters from Southall in London around the rainforest biome at Eden. At first it was too strange for them for much to sink in, but gradually they began to listen and learn. Things really sank home when I pointed out the rosy periwinkle (*Catharanthus roseus*) and explained that it is a miracle cure for childhood leukaemia. One of the group suddenly exclaimed that his young brother had leukaemia, and was now being treated with medicines that were probably from this plant.

As I watch the education staff of the Eden Project working with the many school groups who visit, I feel proud of the vital job we are doing in bringing children and adults into contact with God's world.

Ghillean Prance, former Scientific Director of the Eden Project

Cocoa the Wonder Dog II

No more wet sloppy kisses in the morning; no more keeping my back warm during the night.

No more miserable walks in bone-chilling rain; no more bounding through the snow on a winter's evening.

No more protecting her 'castle' from the daily onslaught by the postal service; no more barking at the invisible dogs parading down her sidewalk. No more squirrel-chasing, cat-aggravating, bouncing-like-Tigger-for-treats adventures; no more lazing in the sunshine on the back deck.

No more trying to fit in my lap because that is what the cat is able to do; no more loud snores on the sofa as we try to watch TV. No more unbridled excitement whenever we touch our shoes or jackets; no more 'I missed you terribly' crying when I walk in the door.

No more looks with eyes that melt the most hardened heart; no more unconditional love that makes every miserable moment of any miserable day disappear.

No more.

Cocoa the Wonder Dog died last night.

It was as unexpected as the Spirit coming down on that first day of Pentecost, and it leaves a hole the size of Hurricane Katrina in my heart.

In the book *All Dogs Go to Heaven* the author talks about heaven overflowing with squirrels, and the dogs all sleeping with God (if that's so, watch out, God: Cocoa likes her space!).

Now, I am commanded to love God with all my Reformed, modern, well-educated mind, which tells me that this is a nice way to try to comfort kids on the death of a beloved pet.

Really?

But ...

... since I am also commanded to love God with all my heart, I will hope for that day to come when Cocoa will come bounding up to me, tail wagging, eyes dancing, ready to go on that walk which will never have to end.

Thom M. Shuman

Hope

The doorbell went, but nobody was there. Just a handwritten note wedged between the storm doors. It was from a neighbour, up the far end of the street. I didn't know her, but she set it out so tenderly upon a scrap of paper.

She said there'd been a posting on Acumfaegovan. That's the Facebook page 'I come from Govan'. Somebody had mentioned that we keep a black-and-white cat. There'd been an accident. The white transit never stopped. As the note had it: 'The wee soul passed away minutes after being hit. I'm so sorry if you are this wee gorgeous cat's owner.'

Mabelle – a name that means 'My beautiful' in French – had first turned up nine years ago. We'd see the odd dead mouse deposited out the back, a gift and visiting card. Soon she took to meowing for attention, day and night. We'd chase her off. But in the morning, she'd be sleeping on the window sill, tail dampened in the rain. She started to befriend my wife Verene when at her morning meditation in the garden. Then one day, I found her inside sitting in an armchair. That was it. We were adopted. Our adopting her just took a little longer. We checked she wasn't microchipped or on a local missing list. Next stop, was the cat flap.

But now, this neighbour's note. Verene was out, thank goodness, and I clutched the scrap of paper like a death certificate as a new and harsh reality took shape, and I dashed around the house and called her name already half-lamenting. There was no sign.

I dashed on up the street. The neighbour was so kind. There seems to be an informal neighbourhood cat watch. Another woman, several streets away, had taken the body to her home for identification and to be claimed.

What struck me, was how part of me observed my own reactions. I had a sense I've known before, as if the greater self from far away watches the machinations of the smaller self. Alongside the emerging grief was a sense of letting go into the Godspace. Ashes to ashes, dust to dust, life to love.

I asked to see where the accident had taken place. A pool of blood dried darkly in the sunshine.

'That's odd,' I said. 'Mabelle doesn't usually venture this far along the road.'

'It might not be yours!' the woman said, hopefully.

'But it will still be somebody's,' I said. I felt the odd dilemma. On the one hand, my small self: 'Let this cup pass.' On the other hand, my greater self: 'Not as I will, but as Thou wilt.'

For if it wasn't ours, who else's? Perhaps a child's dear friend? Perhaps an old folk's sole companion? And those lines in *Four Quartets*, so challenging and pertinent: 'I said to my soul, be still, and wait without hope/For hope would be hope for the wrong thing.' The cross did not deflect the violence of the world. The cross absorbs the violence of the world.

I went back to the house to get a box. I'd take it round to where the dead cat lay in rest. But there was still, in the ordinary sense of the word, hope. I checked the house more carefully. And there she was! Our dear Mabelle, curled up fast asleep in a cupboard.

It turned out that the pet that had been killed had ventured from another street. It was a 15-year-old tom. And who knows? At such a ripe age for a cat, maybe starting to go deaf or blind or worse, a speedy passing can be a blessing in disguise.

When Verene came home, she said she'd seen it being tended as she'd left the house. There was nothing to be done. But the image settled in her deeply. It brought home the compound tragedies of human beings in such localities as Palestine or Ukraine. Our concern was with a cat. But for other folks? Imagine!

Where, then, is God in such times? 'God,' as the poet Hugh

MacDiarmid said, 'if there is one'? What does God survey, from the cross on which the broken world was laid? In times of grief, perhaps we get a glimpse.

'Keep your spirit in hell, and despair not,' said Saint Silouan of Mount Athos. How is that possible? Because, said the Orthodox theologian Paul Evdokimov, 'As deep as the hell in which we find ourselves, it is even more profound to find Christ already there waiting for us.' And he added: 'We can only fall into God and it is God who never despairs.'

Thus, the acceptance. Thus, the ground of deeper hope. 'Be still, and know ...'

One of the most ecological passages in the Bible is chapter 12 of the Book of Job. If you want to make sense of suffering and injustice, advises Job, then ask of the beasts of the field. Or the birds of the air. Or the fishes of the sea.

'Or speak to the earth, and it shall teach thee'! For the hand of God 'hath wrought this'.

God, 'in whose hand is the soul of every living thing, and the breath of all humankind'.

Aye, ask of the beasts, and birds, and fishes, and of the Earth. And might we add: stray alley cats?

Alastair McIntosh

All-embracing compassion

I am reminded of an acquaintance, a woman who has been for me an example of all-embracing compassion. Her job is to look after injured wild birds and animals. Some years ago she looked after five hens. They had come from a factory farm and all their life had been shut in crowded cages with no possibility of moving about naturally. Over time she got to know these hens as individuals. One was shy and stood on the sidelines, another sought out human company and liked its neck stroked. When I spoke to this woman a few months ago she sounded distressed. The previous day one of the hens had died in her arms. 'Her body shuddered and I saw how her gaze turned inwards,' she told me. She had tried heart massage but it hadn't helped.

I was touched by the tenderness in the woman's voice. Think what the human heart is capable of. A hen, a small creature worth very little in the human world; in fact, many of us see hens mainly as egg-producing machines. But this woman's heart was wide open to the hens. She felt what they felt and suffered with them. For her, they were valuable creatures.

Annika Spalde

LITURGY

A litany of blessing

Puppies who think puddles are perfect for baths;
white-muzzlers who chase squirrels in their dreams;
rescuers searching tirelessly through toppled buildings;
companions guiding the sightless;
eyes in whose depths we see God,
soft mouths which open doors;
greeters at the end of dreich days –
ball-chasers and stick-fetchers who get us moving …

For every lab and Lhasa apso,
for every border collie and sheepdog,
for every golden retriever and Great Dane,
for every furry, four-footed best friend:
we give you thanks,
One whose name spelled backwards is dog,
for those companions who shadow us through life;
and we lift their names to you for blessing in this moment:

*(Names of dogs may be spoken aloud, or held in the silence of
people's hearts …)*

Canaries that sing carols at evensong;
finches that lullaby us in the morning;
budgies who talk our ears off;
cockatiels who whistle to catch our attention;
caiques whose eyes twinkle with mischief;
macaws thinking up new ways to trick us;
cockatoos that cling to us 24/7;
parrots with their imperial natures …

For every squawk and tweet,
for every flitter and flutter,
for every feather which brushes our cheek with gentleness,
for every beak which nips us with grace:
we give you thanks,
God of six-winged seraphim,
for the birds who send our hearts soaring;
and we lift their names to you for blessing in this moment:

(Names of birds may be spoken aloud, or held in the silence of people's hearts …)

Mamas who carry their babies to safety by the scruff of their neck;
seniors who sleep their days away;
frightened felines who hide in the smallest spaces;
lappers who purr grace into our depths;
kittens who stalk sunbeams across kitchen floors;
mousers who keep our barns and basements free of problems;
foot-warmers on bitter winter nights;
tree-climbers who thwart every rescue attempt …

For every tiger and tabby, for every Manx and Maltese,
for every tortoiseshell, marmalade and Russian Blue,
for every loquacious Siamese and every soft-spoken Scottish fold,
for every short-hair, long-hair, no-hair and in between:
we give you thanks,
God of gentle contemplation and contentment,
for those feline friends who see us for who we are,
even in the shadows of our lives;
and we lift their names to you for blessing in this moment:

(Names of cats may be spoken aloud, or held in the silence of people's hearts …)

Thoroughbreds moving gently through the morning mist;
Clydesdales with hearts bigger than the sky;
New Forest ponies with history coursing through their veins;
Appaloosas that carry us surefooted along trails;
Tennessee walkers that show us how to persevere;
Welsh cobs that provide joy for children with disabilities …

For puddlers and plodders,
for racers and wild mustangs,
for ponies accepting carrots from children,
and for those who shake their manes
to show us who really is in charge:
we give you thanks,
God of plains and farmlands,
for horses who love and accept us;
and we lift their names to you for blessing in this moment:

(Names of horses may be spoken aloud, or held in the silence of people's hearts …)

For gerbils which teach kids responsibility,
and remind us of the value of smaller spaces;
for hamsters which show us how to compost,
and whose variety reflects the rich diversity of creation;
for cottontails and flop-eared bunnies
whose curiosity knows no bounds;
for leopard geckos and bearded dragons
which show us that it is OK to take time to relax;
for garter snakes, corn snakes and kingsnakes,
for spiders, mice, rats and other critters

others abhor but we adore;
for tropical fish like neon tetras and harlequin rasboras;
for algae eaters, loaches and silvery minnows who drive cats crazy –
for the rich, rainbow variety of your creation
and all those we are given to love and care for by your grace,
we give you thanks, and lift their names to you:

*(Names of pets and different animals may be spoken aloud, or held
in the silence of people's hearts …)*

Thom M. Shuman

Celebrating love for all God's creation:

An all-age communion service for the Feast of Saint Francis (including a blessing of animals)

Notes:

Giving a couple weeks' notice, invite everyone to bring pictures of their pet(s), or a toy stuffed animal of a kind of animal they love *(see Blessing of the animals)*. (One year we did the basics of this service outside on a farm. People brought their pets and we did the blessings individually for each animal. We didn't have communion; instead we had lunch together.)

Have a manger scene including animal figurines set up at the front of the church, near where the children will gather to hear the Christmas story.

Other suitable songs for this service: 'All things bright and beautiful'; 'God of the sparrow'; 'Many and great, O God, are your works'; 'He's got the whole world in his hands'; and any songs that celebrate the many different features of creation in ways that would make St Francis proud!

Introduction:

Leader:

October 4th is called the 'Feast of St Francis'. St Francis was born over 800 years ago in the land we now call Italy. He began life as a wealthy man, travelling through many countries. In his travels, he met many poor people and beggars, and gradually his heart changed. He gave up his business and dedicated his life to God, wandering the roads, dressed as a beggar himself. Soon Francis and his friends began to live and pray together, often travelling around to tell the stories of Jesus wherever they went. The twelve of them, like Jesus' first disciples, were committed to following the teachings of Jesus and walking in his footsteps.

Now, Francis believed we should pay attention to everything God made, not just people who need help but every single thing around us. He thought that the spirit of life within each creature calls to that same spirit of life in all other creatures. That's why we feel sorry for animals when they're young or hurt and need help. And we feel for plants growing, even the ground we walk on and the stars in the sky, because we remember God cares for every precious little detail in the world. In the whole universe, even!

The legend of St Francis tells us that birds and animals would come to him when he was out walking, even when he was preaching to people! Birds would sit on his shoulder, listen to him, sing for him – and for God. And so whenever we remember St Francis, we also remember that every kind of creature – from the birds and wild animals to rocks and stars – has its own way to praise God. Today we can praise God using words written by St Francis himself 800 years ago!

Song: 'All creatures of our God and King' (based on St Francis' 'Canticle of the sun'), various songbooks

We say good morning to God:

Leader:

Good morning, God. We are here to praise you. The sun praises you as the day goes by. The stars praise you with their twinkle. The rain praises you by refreshing the earth. The trees praise you in seeds to grow more trees. Birds praise you in a chirp. Dogs praise you in a yap. How do we praise you, O God? In how we live and what we say and in this time of worship. Praise be to you, O God, from all your many creatures in all our many ways. Amen

We say sorry to God (said together):

Good morning, God.
We have to say sorry
for many things we do without thinking.
Some days we eat too much.
Some days we talk too much.
Some days we don't pay attention
to the birds and the butterflies and the trees
and what they have to say.
We're sorry we spoil places
where we walk with litter
and sometimes forget to do the recycling.
We can make a mess of things, O God.
And we're sorry.

We hear a kind word from Jesus:

Leader:

Dear friends, while it is true we have all made a mess of God's world in some way, it is also true that God forgives us when we own up to what we've done. With Jesus' love we can become new people. So know that we make God glad when we remember to say we're sorry.

St Francis and Christmas Eve:

Leader:

Now St Francis is very important to all of us at Christmas time, though he had nothing to do with St Nicholas. So let's listen to the Christmas story, and I want you to listen very, very carefully. What animals are named in this story?

Listen and count them up.

Bible reading: Luke 2:1–7

Leader:

Now tell me which animals were named in that story?

How many did you count? ...

None! Right!

The way the Bible tells the Christmas story, it mentions no animals. But at Christmas, when we act out the story of Jesus being born in a stable and laid in a manger, we often put animals in our story. In our manger scenes, we usually set a few animals right beside Mary and Joseph and Jesus.

Which animals do we usually put in our manger scenes? ...

Which other animals might have been there at the manger? ...

Now you might be wondering why we're talking about manger scenes on St Francis Day in October. It's because St Francis was the very first person who put together a manger scene, in his little church in Italy one Christmas a long time ago.

To celebrate that Christmas, he gathered many kinds of live animals to join the people playing the parts of Mary and Joseph, the shepherds and Jesus.

St Francis created the very first manger scene to help people remember the story of when Jesus was born. So every time we put up a manger scene at home or act it out in our Christmas service, we should remember St Francis and his love for Jesus! And Francis told the story with the animals at the manger, as if by a miracle, being able to speak on that first Christmas to bring their praise to God and their love to Jesus!

There's an old song that tells us the Christmas story the way St Francis might have, with animals speaking of their love for Jesus.

Song: 'Jesus our brother, kind and good' (various songbooks)

Leader:

Whenever churches celebrate the Feast of St Francis, we remember our love for animals.

What kinds of animals do you love? ... *(Keep a list for the prayers.)*

These days we can also remember animals that need our help: animals in danger because they don't have safe homes to live in, safe water to swim in, enough food to eat.

Today we can ask God to bless all the animals we love and any we've forgotten to mention today.

In some churches, people bring their animals right into church to be blessed with God's love.

We asked you to bring a picture of your pet or a stuffed animal to remember an animal you love. To help us remember all the animals who need God's blessing today.

Invite the children to show their pictures or toys and to say the name of the animal they want to bless. Then look at the photos/animals the adults brought.

Blessing of the animals:

Depending on how much time you wish to take, you can invite people to bring their picture, stuffed animal forward for an individual blessing said by the leader. Or you can invite the children to lift up their pictures and stuffed animals and say the words of blessing all together.

Words of blessing:

God bless you *(say the name of the pet or favourite animal)*, creature of God's own making. Be a blessing to me and to others all the days of your life. Amen.

Leader finishes the act of blessing with a prayer:

God of love, thank you for all the birds and animals, the fish and the frogs, *(adding any animals that the children named earlier)*. All these blessed creatures make Earth interesting and beautiful. Help us take good care of them all for you! Amen.

We offer God our gifts to say thanks.

The offering

Maybe donate the offering to an animal charity.

Listen! You are invited to share the gifts of God from God's table.

Celebrant:

The Feast of St Francis is the feast we share every time we have Communion! Jesus said that people will come from east and west, and from north and south, and sit at table in the kingdom of God.

Today we think of Jesus' followers all over the world, east, west, north and south, sharing bread and wine together just as we do. Today we give thanks for the goodness of the earth which we will taste in the bread and the wine or juice. Whatever we eat and drink in Jesus' name becomes a part of us to help us remember that we are part of everything God made and everything God loves.

Communion song: 'One bread, one body' (various songbooks)

(The offering and the bread and wine are brought to the table.)

Prayer to bless our gifts to God:

God, you are so good to us. We bring you our gifts to say thank you for all you have made and shared with us. Help us share what we have just like St Francis did – in Jesus' name. Amen.

Listen! Learn why we share bread and wine today.

The story of the table:

A long time ago on the night before he died, Jesus gathered with his friends.

He took a loaf of bread and gave thanks to God. He broke the bread and gave it to his friends. Jesus said, 'Think of this bread as my body, for I am giving my life for you. Each time you share bread together, remember I love you.'

After supper Jesus took a cup full of wine and gave thanks to God. He passed that cup to his friends there, saying, 'Drink from this cup, all of you. Think of this wine as my life blood, sealing my promise to love you and forgive you.'

So every time Jesus' friends break bread and share a cup like this in his name, we remember that in him, all things God made hold together.

Great Prayer of thanksgiving (said in a 'rap' style):

Rap:

God, you make us wonder, making all that there is:
We bless you for amazing things – that crawl or go whiz.
We bless you for the moon and stars, for sun up above,
for leaves changing colour and the smells that we love.

Straight talk:

God, we thank you for everything that puts a smile on our face in this good, old earth and in all the worlds beyond this world.

Rap:

Jesus, we're glad you lived a life like ours,
walked in the rain and enjoyed the show'rs.
We're glad you enjoyed a good meal, too
and laughed and cried with your friends like we do.

Straight talk:

Jesus, we thank you that you lived on earth and died on earth
to show us how to find God in the middle of everything that
happens.

Here and now you meet us and feed us at this table
just as all your other friends around the world meet you at theirs.

Rap:

Holy Spirit, breathe on bread and wine on the table
and breathe within us all – to make us able
to remember that we all belong to God,
that you love us deeply, whether perfect or flawed.

Straight talk:

As we taste the bread and sip from your cup,
help us always remember God's love lifts us up.
God's love fills every bite we taste and every breath we take
because Jesus walks beside us every step we make.
We pray in his name.
Amen

Breaking the bread:

Dear friends, this is the Bread of Life. Take this and remember Jesus.

Lifting the cup:

Dear friends, this is the cup of joy.

When you drink your cup, remember Jesus and his love poured out for you.

Sharing the bread and cup (according to local custom)

Sharing the peace of Christ (according to local custom)

Leader: The peace of our Lord Jesus be with you.
And also with you.

Prayer after communion:

God who made us and everything that is,
thank you for caring for us day by day.
We pray for every person who needs your help and healing
and for every other creature your blessing is feeling.
Help us be thankful every day that we live,
grateful for Jesus and the life he gives.
Dear God, we pray you will make us a blessing
so others will see the love we're confessing in Jesus' name.
Amen.

Blessing:

May the grace of our Lord Jesus Christ,
the love of God our maker,
and peace through the Holy Spirit
be with you all.

Nancy Cocks

Creatures worship together:

A service for the blessing of animals

Preparation:

If you are not able to bring an animal, you may wish to bring a toy stuffed animal or a picture of your pet or of an endangered species.

This service could take place in the church but is probably best outdoors or in a barn or outdoor shelter. Most cities will give permission to use a park. Groups like the Royal Society for Prevention of Cruelty to Animals (RSPCA), Animal Welfare and animal shelters are usually happy to participate. Suggested dates are St Francis Day, World Animal Day, Earth Day, or any nice summer's afternoon. Or you might have an online service.

Space is needed between the animals to provide a comfortable experience. All animals should be on a lead or in a carrier or pen for the safety of animals and people.

Consider using information about animal welfare in Christian history: St Francis, the patron saint of animals; St Martin de Porres, who set up the first animal shelter after living on the street and seeing so many strays; John Wesley, who cared deeply for animals, and preached that all animals would join us in heaven; Anna Sewell, a Quaker, who wrote *Black Beauty* to expose the cruel conditions of working horses in London.

This is a great time to reach out to the community around the church in a relaxed setting. Advertise the service and invite people to bring chairs or blankets to sit on. You might provide a table for pictures or symbols of animals. Photos of nature could be projected on a screen; a CD of nature sounds could be played as people gather. Songs and readings are suggested but may be omitted.

'Doggy bags' could be prepared with treats for pets. (Empty doggy bags should be available for any accidents!) You might choose to have St Francis medals or animal bookmarks for people to take with them as a memento.

Prelude: 'All God's creatures got a place in the choir'

Welcome:

But ask the animals, and they will teach you,
the birds of the air, and they will tell you;
ask the plants of the earth and they will teach you,
and the fish of the sea will declare to you …
(Job 12:7–10)

In the Creator's hand is the life of every living thing.

Call to worship for all God's creatures:

Are any among you in need of a blessing?
Call your human companions and have them pray over you,
and bless you in the name of the Lord.
The prayers of those who care for you will bless you,
and their healing touch will lift you up.

May our Creator bless you with love and understanding.
We will confess our harmful ways and pray for you.
May the One who holds creation near, bless us and guide us,
that we may be a blessing to all creatures great and small.

(or)

Come, let us gather together
and praise our Creator for life and love.

Let us bless the creatures in our care
and all those who have gone before us.

Passing the paws of peace:

Peace be with you and all our animal friends.

(All creatures are greeted and/or petted.)

Song: 'All creatures great and small'
(Barking encouraged)

Prayer of thanks and forgiveness:
(for two voices, or with all folk responding)

Creator God, you have made a beautiful world
filled with wonder and surprise!
We adore all you have made.

Creator God, you have gifted us with the blessing of animals,
those in the wild, those on farms, those in our own homes.
Oh, how we love our cats and dogs.

Creator God, you brought life into being in a world
we could not imagine,
all creatures and animals near us and around the world.
Oh, how you amaze us.

We thank you for the abundance of life,
for birds and bees and the vastness of your creation.
Oh, how we give you thanks.

We thank you for the gift of animal companions:
for the joy they bring us,
for their unconditional love and forgiveness

which teach us about you,
for the benefits they are to our health and to our spirit.
We give you thanks.

And yet, we know
that we have not always been faithful caretakers
of animals and the environment;
forgive us when we have neglected what you have created,
forgive us when we have not loved what you love.
God is love.
Through Christ our sins are forgiven.
Thanks be to God.
Amen

Song: 'All creatures of our God and King'
(Meows appreciated)

Scripture responses:

Adapted from Psalm 104

O Lord, how wonderful are your works!
In wisdom you have made all things;
the earth is full of your creatures.
Yonder is the sea, great and wide,
creeping things innumerable there are,
living things both great and small.
They all look to you to give them their food in due season;
when you open your hand,
they are filled with good things.
When you send forth your Spirit, they are created;
and you renew the face of the earth.
May the glory of the Lord endure forever.

(or)

Adapted from Matthew 6:25–26

Therefore, I tell you, do not worry about your life, what you will eat or what you will drink, or about your body, what you will wear. Is not life more than food, and the body more than clothing? Look at the birds of the air: they neither sow nor reap nor gather into barns, and yet your Creator feeds them all.

Reflection (and/or share readings or personal reflections about animals):

I love sheep. The farmers at my church used to laugh when I said that because they said if I knew sheep like they do I wouldn't say that. But I still love sheep.

When I lived in northern England, I saw sheep everywhere. I used to go walking on Pendle Hill, which was only a few miles from the manse, and sheep were always grazing there. I went there to let go of stress and worries about ministry and to just walk and pray, and I still go there every time I visit.

Pendle Hill is on the moors, which means there are no trees, just grass and sheep. The wind is always blowing but you can't really tell from which direction it is coming. Sometimes it feels like I'm surrounded by the Spirit of God. The wind encircles me on all sides and seems to hold me as I walk. It's often raining or drizzling up on Pendle, but that's the best time to walk: a mist or fog settles over the hills and makes everything seem as though the mystery of God is very close. Prayer is effortless when I am there; walking in the mist and wind is prayer. Often while I am walking the mist is so thick, I can't see the path ahead, and suddenly, the face of a sheep appears right in front of me. We both stop for a moment and staring into each other's eyes is just the blessing I need. Then we go our separate ways.

I carry this memory with me because it is so vivid and reminds me that God's blessings come in many forms, from nature and from all the creatures we meet on our journey. This is one of the reasons why I love sheep.

Let us bless the animals we love and who bless us.

Song: 'All things bright and beautiful'
(All animal noises acceptable)

Invitation:

Today we come together to give thanks for God's creation
and to ask God's blessings:
for peace in our world and in our lives;
for all animals, those close to us and those in the wild;
for people involved in animal welfare and conservation work;
for farmers who care for animals,
that all animals may be treated with respect;
for veterinarians and animal hospitals
and all who care for animals;
for the strays on our streets;
for grieving pet owners: may warm memories heal their grief.
May we be a blessing to all creation and all living creatures.

Blessing of the animals:

Animals may be brought forward row by row in order to be blessed; or ministers and assistants may circulate around the animals. Ask the name of the animal, place hand on the animal (if appropriate), and bless the animal with the following, or other, words. Alternatively, all animals may be blessed at once.

For online services, bring your animal, or picture, or toy stuffed animal to the screen.

(Name of animal, e.g., Shawn),
you were created by God, and you are loved by God.
May God's blessing be on you and your human family
that you may experience joy and companionship
throughout your life,
and continue to be a blessing to each other.
Amen

(or)

(Name of animal), God bless you with peace and love in this life and forever. Amen

Unison prayer after blessing:

We bless all animals, and remember our animal companions who are no longer with us.
We give thanks for the gifts they give us
and all the ways they enrich and bless our lives.
May our Creator continue to care for us and them.
Amen

Song: 'Sing the Almighty power of God'
(All animals and their companions make a joyful noise)

Sending forth:

Go out into the world,
bark and scratch, meow and purr,
and love one another.
Care for each other,
and be blessings of hope,
that all creation may know God's love.

Postlude: 'The creatures we love' (by Amanda Udis-Kessler)

Rebeka Maples

A lamentation and prayer of contrition
to the whole of creation

1   *[To the heavenly hosts and the Holy Ghost]* We have painted over the canvas of your starry skies

2   With neon and floodlights blinding us to our place in your creation.

3   Without sight, we can no longer see and hear your morning stars singing together.

4   Our hearts have grown cold and closed to the pulsars of eternal love.

5   We have inflicted violence on your creation, grievous wounds on your body.

6   We have monetised the commons and disavowed our kinship with all living things.

7   We enslaved non-human beings and severed their ties to the land.

8   We have denied water to the thirsty, bread to the hungry, shelter to the refugee.

9   We abandoned belief and made graven images to worship Mammon.

10   We no longer marvel at your bow in the sky and have broken humanity into petty pieces.

11   The colours in your rainbow would remind us how much you love diversity

12   And how each dewdrop glistens with potential in the unfolding dance of life.

For our sins against the biomes, genomes and creature homes, forgive us our trespasses, have mercy upon our souls.

13 *[To the cryosphere]* With your breath the ice is formed and watery expanses are frozen. *(Job 47:10)*

14 We have melted your cryosphere so that the great winds across the lands and ocean currents falter

15 Bringing drought and famine and cruel blasts of heat and cold against the creatures.

For our sins against the biomes, genomes and creature homes, forgive us our trespasses, have mercy upon our souls.

16 *[To the forests]* Woodlands once flourished like the forests of Lebanon *(Ps 72:16)* and the trees sang for joy. *(Ps 96:12)*

17 But now the towering trees of the forest cathedrals are felled to make toilet paper, with few left to rebuild your Temples.

18 The land is now desolate, stumps burning, the soil washing away with the monsoon, a wasteland bereft of creatures.

For our sins against the biomes, genomes and creature homes, forgive us our trespasses, have mercy upon our souls.

19 *[To the grasslands]* Where the wilderness grasslands over-flowed, the hills were clothed with gladness. *(Ps 65:12)*

20 But now we weep and mourn for the grasslands on the mountain; we sing a mournful song for the pastures in the wilderness.

21 Because they are so scorched no one travels through them;
the sound of livestock is no longer heard there.

22 Even the birds in the sky and the wild animals in the fields
have fled and are gone. *(Jer 9:10)*

**For our sins against the biomes, genomes and creature
homes, forgive us our trespasses, have mercy upon our
souls.**

23 *[To the deserts]* You brought us into a good land, with
brooks of water, fountains that spring out of valleys and
hills. *(Deut 8:7)*

24 Where the desert and the dry land rejoiced, celebrated and
blossomed like crocuses. *(Isa 35:1)*

25 And we have become like a shrub in the desert, trying to
grow in a salt land where nothing can live. *(Jer 17:6)*

**For our sins against the biomes, genomes and creature
homes, forgive us our trespasses, have mercy upon our
souls.**

26 *[To the freshwater and wetlands]* You caused springs to gush
forth into rivers that flow between the mountains. *(Ps 104:10)*

27 And the rivers clapped their hands and the mountains
shouted together for joy. *(Ps 98:8)*

28 We lived like a tree planted by the rivers of water that brought
forth fruit in its season, and its leaves did not wither. *(Ps 1:3)*

29 Until the rivers were aflame with our petrochemicals and
our fertilisers poisoned your water creatures.

**For our sins against the biomes, genomes and creature
homes, forgive us our trespasses, have mercy upon our
souls.**

30 *[To the oceans]* You made the sea great and broad, with swarms of life without number, creatures both small and great. *(Ps 104:25)*

31 We have plundered your bounty, and polluted your seas with plastic and chemicals.

32 The oceans' great creatures groan and beach themselves from the noise pollution of our invasive vessels.

For our sins against the biomes, genomes and creature homes, forgive us our trespasses, have mercy upon our souls.

33 *[To the firstborn peoples]* We ask forgiveness of our brothers and sisters, the Native Peoples

34 For bringing disease and death upon their totem clans, communities and cities.

35 We have plundered their sacred groves and disturbed their ancestors in their rest

36 And denigrated and desecrated their ancient knowledge and wisdom.

37 We confess that it has taken centuries for our binary science

38 To confirm that their beliefs and values were in harmony with the whole creation.

39 And that, as they warned us, we have become possessed by our possessions.

40 Intoxicated with hubris, greed and selfishness.

41 Convinced of our separateness and superiority.

For our sins against the biomes, genomes and creature homes, forgive us our trespasses, have mercy upon our souls.

42 We repent and seek redemption.

43 With humility we pray for healing and commit our labours to peace.

44 May our faith going forward be as a grain of mustard seed, planted in your garden,

45 Growing into a Tree of Life, that the birds of the air will make their homes once again in its branches. *(Lk 13:19)*

46 May we be keepers of the commons, in the Nowness of your vast and beautiful creation

47 That we might come to be in right relations with all creatures walking the twofold way that carries us home to you, the Creator *(Wis 13:5)*

48 And perfuses your stillness throughout our hearts forever.

49 In your name, our loving landlord, we pray and we act in community.

50 You above all and others above ourselves.

51 We could say more but could never say enough; let the final word be: Saleh. *(Sir 43:27)*

For our sins against the biomes, genomes and creature homes, forgive us our trespasses, have mercy upon our souls. Saleh.

Richard A. Nisbett

The 51 lines of the prayer commemorate 51 Earth Days since the original Earth Day in 1970. (This piece was written in 2021.)

Sources and acknowledgements

'Christmas 2020' appeared in the autumn 2020, Issue 1, edition of *Kith Review*, Cinnamon Press. 'Winter's breakfast guests' and 'Words like birds' are from *Not Sonnets*, Cinnamon Press, Bonnie Thurston, 2022. Used by permission of Bonnie Thurston and Cinnamon Press.

'Bless to me my dog' – by Joy Mead, from *A Book of Blessings and How to Write Your Own*, Ruth Burgess (Ed.), Wild Goose Publications, 2001.

'Bless my cat', by Rosie Miles, from *A Book of Blessings and How to Write Your Own*, Ruth Burgess (Ed.), Wild Goose Publications, 2001.

'For ordinary, wonderful things', by Richard Sharples, adapted from a prayer in *A Heart for Creation: Worship Resources and Reflections on the Environment*, Chris Polhill (Ed.), Wild Goose Publications, 2010.

'St Hubert and the stag', by Annie Heppenstall, from *Healer's Tree: A Bible-based Resource on Ecology, Peace & Justice*, Annie Heppenstall, Wild Goose Publications, 2011.

'An incarnate God', by Annika Spalde, from *A Heart on Fire: Living as a Mystic in Today's World*, Annika Spalde, Wild Goose Publications, 2010.

'Ask the animals', by Ghillean Prance, from *Go to the Ant: Reflections on Biodiversity and the Bible*, Ghillean Prance, Wild Goose Publications, 2013.

'Cocoa the Wonder Dog I', by Thom M. Shuman, from *Compan-*

ions on the Journey: A Blessing of Pets and Animals Who Are a Part of Our Lives, Thom M. Shuman, Wild Goose Publications, 2015.

'Scooby', by Tom Gordon, adapted from *Welcoming Each Wonder: More Contemporary Stories for Reflection*, Tom Gordon, Wild Goose Publications, 2010.

'God's world', by Ghillean Prance, from *Go to the Ant: Reflections on Biodiversity and the Bible*, Ghillean Prance, Wild Goose Publications, 2013.

'All-embracing compassion', by Annika Spalde, from *A Heart on Fire: Living as a Mystic in Today's World*, Annika Spalde, Wild Goose Publications, 2010.

'A litany of blessing', by Thom M. Shuman, from *Companions on the Journey: A Blessing of Pets and Animals Who Are a Part of Our Lives*, Thom M. Shuman, Wild Goose Publications, 2015.

Celebrating love for all God's creation: An all-age communion service for the Feast of Saint Francis (including a blessing of animals), by Nancy Cocks, Wild Goose Publications download, 2018.

'A lamentation and prayer of contrition to the whole of creation', by Richard A. Nisbett, from *Living Faithfully in a Time of Creation*, Kathy Galloway & Katharine M. Preston, Wild Goose Publications, 2021.

ABOUT THE CONTRIBUTORS

Rodney Aist is the course director at St George's College, Jerusalem. He is an associate member of the Iona Community and author of *Pilgrim Spirituality: Defining Pilgrimage Again for the First Time*, Cascade Books, 2022.

Nancy Cocks is a retired Presbyterian minister with research interests in children's spirituality and storytelling.

Brian Ford: 'I am a retired schoolteacher. When I'm not writing poetry I'm involved in various types of Christian work, and I enjoy gardening, guitar-playing and mosaic-making.'

Tom Gordon is a retired Church of Scotland minister and former Hospice Chaplain. He writes extensively, and publishes a daily blog on https://swallowsnestnet.wordpress.com

Annie Heppenstall brings the inspiration she finds in nature to all her writing and her wider work as a therapeutic community garden chaplain and as a tutor for an educational charity specialising in inclusive, interfaith ministry training.

Janet Lees is a member of the Lay Community of St Benedict, a writer and a long-distance walker who loves to interact with animals and other species with whom we share the planet. You can follow her on Twitter/X @Bambigoesforth.

Glendon Macaulay is a retired Church of Scotland minister who, in all seriousness, once conducted a burial service for a gerbil named Elvis. The children of Elvis' family were sorely grieving, having lost a much-loved pet and dear friend.

Rebeka Maples: 'As clergy and director of spiritual formation, I continue to seek the sacred through working with fabric, writing, walking and quiet moments in nature. I draw inspiration from the beauty of creation and the comfort of all God's creatures, great and small.'

Alastair McIntosh grew up in a crofting community in the Isle of Lewis. A human ecologist, he is an associate member of the Iona Community, an honorary professor at the University of Glasgow, and author of books including *Soil and Soul*, *Poacher's Pilgrimage* and *Parables of Northern Seed* from Wild Goose Publications.

Joy Mead is a poet and a member of the Iona Community.

Rosie Miles is a former English Literature academic and now runs her own poetry workshops and retreats. She has also retrained as a professional gardener.

Richard A. Nisbett is an anthropologist, ecologist and epidemiologist who worked in the Global South on biodiversity conservation and community health. An associate member of the Iona Community, he has served as Convener of their CCN Eco.

Neil Paynter is an editor, writer and late-night piano player.

Professor Sir *Ghillean Prance*, D.Phil., FRS, VMH, botanist and former Director of the Royal Botanic Gardens, Kew (1988–1999), has led 39 botanical expeditions to Amazonia and collected over 350 new species of plants. He is the author of 29 books and 530 scientific and general papers in taxonomy, ethnobotany, economic botany, conservation and ecology.

Katherine Rennie is a member of the Iona Community. She is a retired solicitor and family mediator.

Richard Sharples is a Methodist minister who loves cycling, pilgrimage, gardening and the arts. He is married to Biddy and they are both members of the Iona Community.

Thom M. Shuman continues to practise the daily discipline of writing. He also continues to be an advocate for the vulnerable in our world.

Annika Spalde is a deacon in the Church of Sweden. She is the author of many books, including *Every Creature a Word of God: Compassion for Animals as Christian Spirituality* (with Pelle Strind-lund), Wild Goose Publications.

Bonnie Thurston: 'These birds are my "pets" (along with chip-munks, the occasional raccoon who stumbles through, and once in a while, a doe who eats apple slices out of my hand).' For-merly a university and seminary professor Bonnie Thurston is the author of many books, including *From Darkness to Eastering*, Wild Goose Publications, 2017.

Wild Goose Publications, the publishing house of the Iona Community established in the Celtic Christian tradition of Saint Columba, produces books, e-books, CDs and digital downloads.

- holistic spirituality
- social justice
- political, peace and environmental issues
- healing and wellbeing
- fiction and poetry
- innovative approaches to worship
- song in worship, including the work of the Wild Goose Resource Group
- material for meditation and reflection

Visit our website at
www.ionabooks.com
for details of all our products and online sales